Note to parents, carers and teachers

Read it yourself is a series of modern stories, favourite characters and traditional tales written in a simple way for children who are learning to read. The books can be read independently or as part of a guided reading session.

Each book is carefully structured to include many high-frequency words vital for first reading. The sentences on each page are supported closely by pictures to help with understanding, and to offer lively details to talk about.

The books are graded into four levels that progressively introduce wider vocabulary and longer stories as a reader's ability and confidence grows.

Ideas for use

- Begin by looking through the book and talking about the pictures. Has your child heard this story before?

- Help your child with any words he does not know, either by helping him to sound them out or supplying them yourself.

- Developing readers can be concentrating so hard on the words that they sometimes don't fully grasp the meaning of what they're reading. Answering the puzzle questions at the end of the book will help with understanding.

For more information and advice on Read it yourself and book banding, visit **www.ladybird.com/readityourself**

Book
Band
7

Level 2 is ideal for children who have received some reading instruction and can read short, simple sentences with help.

Special features:

Frequent repetition of main story words and phrases

Short, simple sentences

Everyone in Berk was very happy.

It was time for Snoggletog, the big dragon party.

6

Careful match between story and pictures

Hiccup and Toothless were flying from Berk.

They saw some other dragons going by.

"Where are they going off to?" said Hiccup.

Large, clear type

8

9

Educational Consultant: Geraldine Taylor
Book Banding Consultant: Kate Ruttle

LADYBIRD BOOKS

UK | USA | Canada | Ireland | Australia
India | New Zealand | South Africa

Ladybird Books is part of the Penguin Random House group of companies
whose addresses can be found at global.penguinrandomhouse.com.

www.penguin.co.uk   www.puffin.co.uk   www.ladybird.co.uk

First published 2016
This edition published 2017
001

Printed in China

A CIP catalogue record for this book is available from the British Library

ISBN: 978-0-241-24975-8

All correspondence to:
Ladybird Books
Penguin Random House Children's
80 Strand, London WC2R 0RL

The Great
DRAGON
Party

Adaptation written by
Ellen Philpott

Everyone in Berk was very happy.

It was time for Snoggletog, the big dragon party.

Hiccup and Toothless were flying from Berk.

They saw some other dragons going by.

"Where are they going off to?" said Hiccup.

"Help! My helmet!"
said Hiccup.

His helmet had come off,
but there was no time
to get it back.

Everyone in Berk was sad.

"All the dragons are flying away," they said.

"Now this Snoggletog will be no good."

said Astrid. "We will make presents!"

Hiccup was about to help, but then Toothless went away, too.

Now Hiccup was sad.

"Where is Toothless?"
said Hiccup.

He went in the barn and
saw another dragon.

The dragon took Hiccup
and they went flying after
the other dragons.

"Hiccup! Where are you going?" said Astrid.

Then she got some dragon eggs from the barn.

"They will make good surprise Snoggletog presents," she said.

Hiccup and the dragon got to an island.

Then Hiccup saw all the dragons!

They had come to the island to have babies.

"So this is where you are!" said Hiccup.

The dragon eggs were about to hatch.

When they hatched, the eggs went *BANG!*

"So that is why all the dragons have to get away from Berk," said Hiccup.

Back in Berk, Astrid took her presents to everyone.

It was a very big surprise when they hatched!

BANG! BANG!

After that, there was
another happy surprise.

The dragons took their
babies and went back
to Berk for the party.

"The dragons are back!"
said everyone. "Now
Snoggletog will be good!"

When it was the party, Hiccup saw Toothless come back.

Hiccup was very happy. "My helmet! You went back for it!" he said.

"Happy Snoggletog, everyone!"

How much do you remember about the story of The Great Dragon Party? Answer these questions and find out!

- **What falls off Hiccup's head when he is out flying?**

- **What does Astrid find in the barn?**

- **Why do the dragons go to the island?**

- **What do the dragon eggs do when they hatch?**

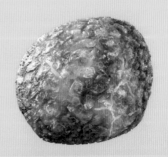

Look at the pictures and match them to the story words.

Hiccup

Toothless

Astrid

eggs

helmet

Tick the books you've read!

Level 1

☐ ☐ ☐ ☐ ☐

☐ ☐ ☐ ☐ ☐

Level 2

☐ ☐ ☐ ☐ ☐

☐ ☐ ☐ ☐ ☐

Level 3

☐ ☐ ☐ ☐ ☐

Level 4

☐ ☐ ☐ ☐ ☐